# My Safety

By

Kirsty Holmes

## Crabtree Publishing Company
www.crabtreebooks.com
1-800-387-7650

**Published in Canada**
**Crabtree Publishing**
616 Welland Avenue
St. Catharines, ON
L2M 5V6

**Published in the United States**
**Crabtree Publishing**
PMB 59051
350 Fifth Ave, 59th Floor
New York, NY 10118

Published by Crabtree Publishing Company in 2018

First Published by Book Life in 2018

**Author:** Kirsty Holmes

**Editors:** Holly Duhig, Janine Deschenes

**Design:** Danielle Jones

**Proofreader:** Petrice Custance

**Production coordinator and**
**   prepress technician (interior):** Margaret Amy Salter

**Prepress technician (covers):** Ken Wright

**Print coordinator:** Margaret Amy Salter

Printed in the USA/012018/BG20171102

**Photographs**
Abbreviations: l-left, r-right, b-bottom,
t-top, c-centre, m-middle.

Front cover – Asier Romero. 2 – dsy88. 4 – wavebreakmedia. 5 – Ilike. 6 – Bigbubblebee99. 7 – Monkey Business Images. 8 – Marcos Mesa Sam Wordley. 9 – Grekov's. 10 –ZephyrMedia. 11 – Kamira. 12 – Ermolaev Alexander. 13 – Creativa Images. 14 – sirtravelalot. 15l – michaeljung, 15c – RTimages, 15r – wavebreakmedia. 16 – Newman Studio. 17 – Dieter Hawlan. 18 – nw10photography. 19 – Idea Studio. 20tr – Butterfly Hunter, 20tc – Andy Dean Photography, 20tr – FabrikaSimf, 20bl – Fotofermer. 21 – Yuliya Evstratenko. 22l – Syda Production, 22c – Solid Web Designs LTD, 22r – michaeljung. 23l – kurhan, 23c – Flashon Studio, 23r – Voyagerix. Images are courtesy of Shutterstock.com. With thanks to Getty Images, Thinkstock Photo and iStockphoto.

**Library and Archives Canada Cataloguing in Publication**

Holmes, Kirsty Louise, author
        My beliefs / Kirsty Holmes.

(Our values)
Includes index.
Issued in print and electronic formats.
ISBN 978-0-7787-4727-7 (hardcover).--
ISBN 978-0-7787-4742-0 (softcover).--
ISBN 978-1-4271-2080-9 (HTML)

        1. Respect for persons--Juvenile literature. 2. Respect--Juvenile literature. 3. Freedom of religion--Juvenile literature. 4. Values--Juvenile literature. 5. Toleration--Juvenile literature. I. Title.

BJ1533.R4H65 2018          j179'.9          C2017-906915-2
                                                              C2017-906916-0

**Library of Congress Cataloging-in-Publication Data**

CIP available at the Library of Congress

# Contents

Words that look like **this** can be found in the glossary on page 24.

# Staying Safe

**Look around you. What interesting things can you see?**

It can be fun to explore the world around you. There are many things to learn about and experience, or take part in.

It is very important to know which things in the world around us are safe, and which things are not safe.

If we are not safe, we could get hurt.

# Accidents

If you have a small accident, you might need just a bandage.

We can get hurt if we do something that is not safe. This is called an accident.

Sometimes, we need to go to the doctor or to a **hospital** when we have accidents.

Doctors and nurses look after us in hospitals.

7

# At Home

Always make sure an adult helps you in the kitchen.

Home is a safe place. We still need to be **careful** with some things, though.

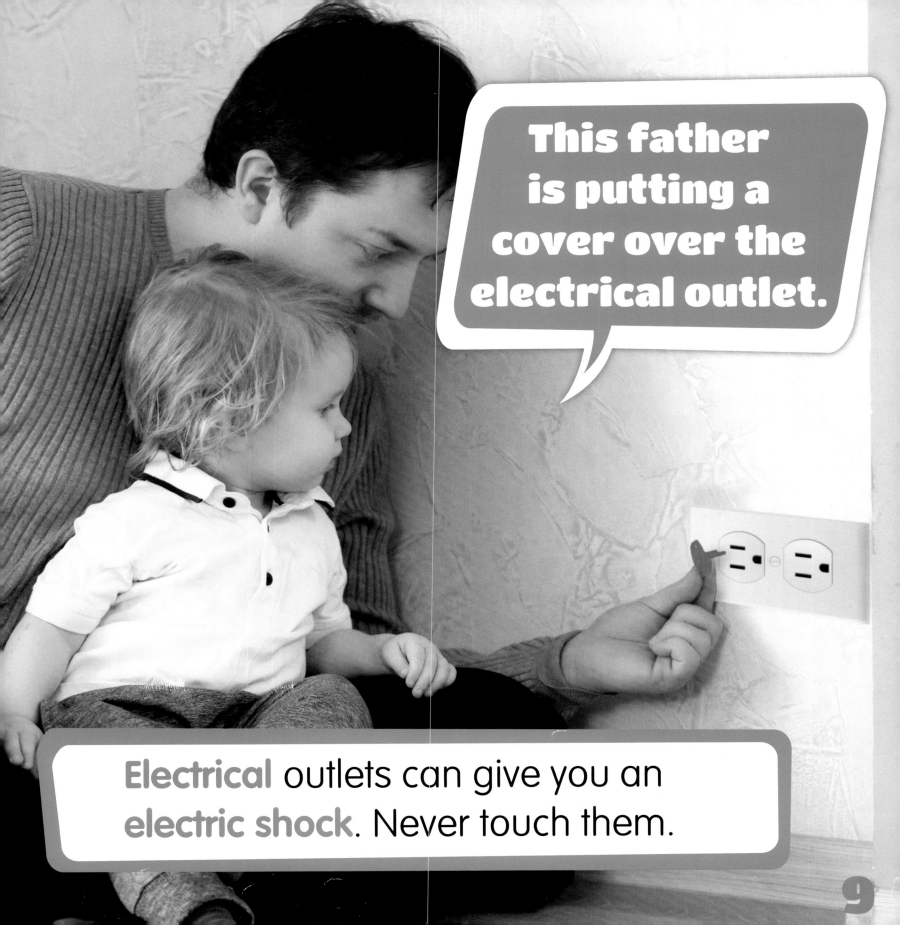

This father is putting a cover over the electrical outlet.

Electrical outlets can give you an electric shock. Never touch them.

If you have a pet at home, treat it with **respect**. Never hurt your pet, or it might bite or scratch you.

Animals are living things, just like you! Treat them kindly.

# Out and About

It is fun to ride a bike or scooter, but falling off can hurt. Be careful and only ride at a safe speed. Always wear a helmet. Other items, such as knee pads, also help you stay safe.

It is important to be safe around water. An adult must be present for any activity you do near water, such as swimming or boating.

Life jackets can help you float.

Holding hands with an adult helps us to not get lost.

Always stay with an adult when you are in a busy place, such as a park or shopping mall.

Wearing a coat protects you from the cold.

If you play outdoors, stay safe by wearing the right clothing. Wear warm clothing if it is cold outside. Wear light clothing if it is hot.

# Road Safety

A crossing guard makes sure you cross the road safely.

Look out for cars and other **vehicles** when you are near roads. Always cross the road with an adult. Never cross on your own.

Before crossing the road, you must always stop, look, and listen for vehicles coming.

The red hand means stop.

A white or green person means go.

Crosswalks help us cross the street safely. They have lines on the ground to show us where to walk, and lights that tell us when to walk.

18

Seat belts keep us safe when we ride in vehicles.

When you are in a vehicle, you must sit in your car seat and keep your seat belt on.

# Don't Touch!

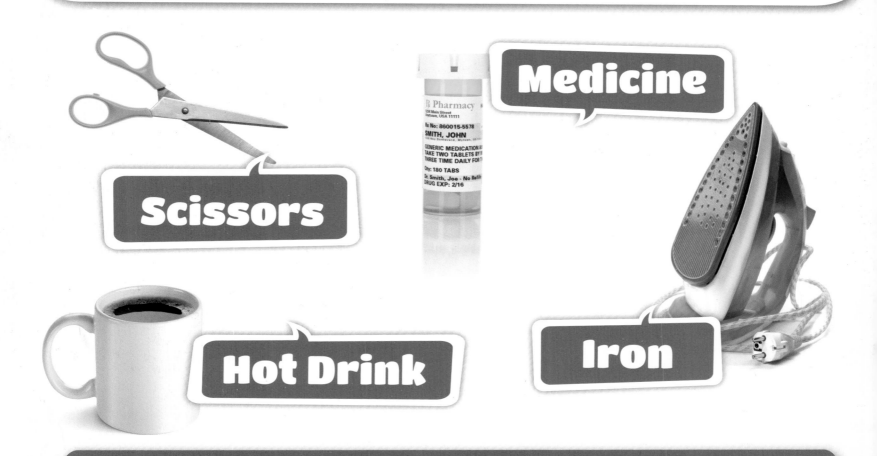

Scissors

Medicine

Hot Drink

Iron

If an adult tells you not to touch something, listen to them. Many things may look interesting, but are not safe to touch.

# People Who Keep Us Safe

Parent

Doctor

Police Officer

Some people have the special job of keeping us safe. You can ask them for help if you are hurt or do not feel safe.

How do you think these people keep us safe? Talk about this with an adult.

Teacher

Lifeguard

Firefighter

23

# Glossary

**careful**    Making sure to avoid getting hurt

**electric shock**    An accident caused by electricity running through your body

**electrical**    Something that uses electricity to work

**float**    To rest on and stay above water

**hospital**    A place where sick or injured people are cared for

**respect**    A feeling that someone or something is good and important

**seat belt**    A strap that holds someone in a car seat

**vehicles**    Machines used for transporting people

# Index